This Little Tiger book belongs to:

_____

_____

_____

For Ems, Mum and Dad and for Adèle

LITTLE TIGER PRESS
An imprint of Magi Publications
1 The Coda Centre, 189 Munster Road,
London SW6 6AW
www.littletigerpress.com

First published in Great Britain 2004
by Little Tiger Press, London
This edition published 2010

ISBN 978-1-84895-176-1
Printed in China
2 4 6 8 10 9 7 5 3 1

newton

and the big mess

by Rory Tyger

LITTLE TIGER PRESS

PITTER PATTER! PLIP PLOP!

It was raining.

"Look, Snappy!" said Newton. "Lots of big puddles to jump in. What fun! Let's go splish-splashing. I'll get my coat and boots and then we'll be ready."

Newton found his raincoat
and umbrella hanging by the door.
Then he found . . .

. . . one rubber boot.

"That's strange, Snappy," he said.
"I'm sure I was wearing both boots
last time I went splashing!
Wherever can the
other one be?"

Newton looked for
his boot all over the
house. He looked
in the toybox.

He looked under the bed.
He even looked in the bed!
But he couldn't find it anywhere!

"I know!" said Newton.
"It must be in the cupboard
under the stairs."

Newton pulled open the cupboard
door a little bit and peered inside.
It was very dark. He saw a huge
jumble of shapes.

"Don't be scared, Snappy,"
he said. "I'll turn on the light."

Newton opened
the door and gasped.
"Oh my!" he said.
"Come on, Snappy,
I'm going to need
your help!"

Newton waded into the
clutter and started searching
for his missing rubber boot.

Newton searched deeper and deeper in the cupboard, flinging things over his shoulder as he went.

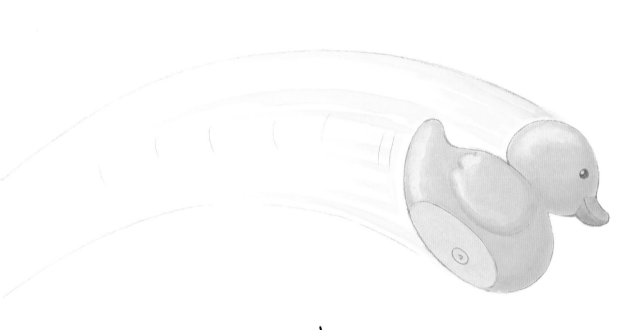

"Bat!" WHEE! BONK!

"Ooooh! Stinks! A smelly sock!" WHEE! SPLAT!
"Sorry, Snappy!"

"Rubber duck!" WHEE! BOING! BOUNCE!

Newton stopped and held up a shiny
red rain hat.

"I thought I'd lost that!" he said.

At last, in the deepest, darkest part of the
cupboard, Newton found the missing boot.
"Hooray! I knew it was here," he cried.
"Now, let's go quickly before the
rain stops and
the puddles
go away!"

Newton pulled on his boot and looked at his shiny red feet.

Then he looked around him. "What a mess we've made, Snappy!" he said. "But there's no time to clear up now. We can do it later."

Newton threw everything
back into the cupboard as
quickly as he could.
He leaned against the door
and, with a huge heave,
he shut it.
   "Right then, Snappy.
Let's go splashing!"
Newton cried.

"Snappy? . . .

   . . . Snappy?"

Newton looked around, but he guessed
where Snappy must be – he'd stuffed
him into the cupboard
by mistake!

Newton looked anxiously at the door.
There was only one thing to do.

"Don't worry, Snappy. I'm coming
to rescue you."

Newton took a deep breath and
turned the door handle as
gently as he could . . .

WHAM!
BANG!
CRASH!

Everything came tumbling
out of the cupboard, covering
Newton like a huge wave.
"Oops!" said Newton.
"I thought that might
happen!"

As Newton scrambled to his feet he saw
just what he needed. It was a shiny helmet.

"Emergency! Newton to the rescue!" he called.
And he set to work, clearing the cupboard.

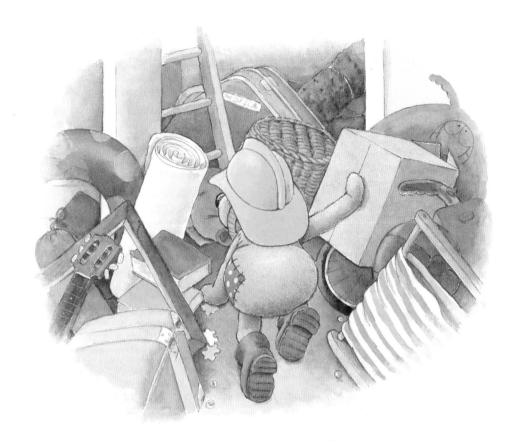

CRASH! BANG! CLATTER! CLUNK!

Soon there were only a few things left in the
cupboard and Newton was getting worried.
He was sure that Snappy was lost forever.

Newton picked up an old coat and was about to throw it away when he spotted something.

"Snappy? Is that you?" he asked. Newton looked closer and sure enough, there was Snappy.

"Hooray!"

Newton gave Snappy the biggest hug. "Poor Snappy," he said. "And all because of this big, big mess. I don't EVER want to lose you again."

Then something amazing happened.
Newton started to put things away, and he
didn't stop until everything was neat and in
its proper place. "Now, Snappy," he said,

"let's go splashing!"

And so they did!

More fantastic reads from Little Tiger Press!

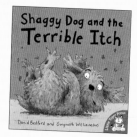
Shaggy Dog and the Terrible Itch
David Bedford and Gwyneth Williamson

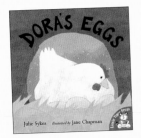
DORA'S EGGS
Julie Sykes   illustrated by Jane Chapman

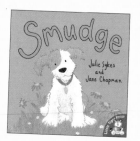
Smudge
Julie Sykes and Jane Chapman

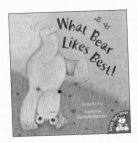
What Bear Likes Best!
Alison Ritchie   illustrated by Dubravka Kolanovic

When will it be Spring?
CATHERINE WALTERS

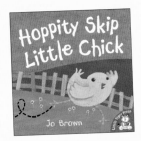
Hoppity Skip Little Chick
Jo Brown

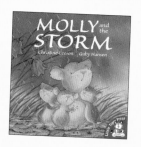
MOLLY and the STORM
Christine Leeson   Gaby Hansen

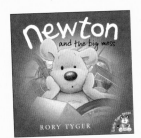
newton and the big mess
RORY TYGER

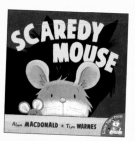
SCAREDY MOUSE
Alan MACDONALD ★ Tim WARNES

For information regarding any of the above titles or for our catalog, please contact us:
Little Tiger Press, 1 The Coda Centre, 189 Munster Road, London SW6 6AW, UK
Tel: +44 (0)20 7385 6333 • Fax: +44 (0)20 7385 7333 E-mail: info@littletiger.co.uk • www.littletigerpress.com